DEDICATION

I'd like to dedicate this book to my daughter Hattie Bowles.
To love you and experience your life has been the greatest gift.
You are the shining light to all things in my journey.

THANKS

Kylie and Hattie Bowles, Jerry and Janis Bowles, Zac Brown
Band and families, ROAR, Governor Nathan Deal, First Lady
Sandra Deal, Commissioner Amy M. Jacobs, Liz Young,
Tom Bledsoe, Joanna Davidovich, and Anna McKean.

BEHIND THE
LITTLE RED DOOR

WRITTEN BY **Coy Bowles**
ILLUSTRATED BY **Joanna Davidovich**

What's behind the **little red door**?

The one in the corner
next to the floor.

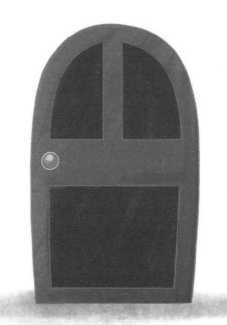

There's a world in there I'd love to explore.

What's behind the
little red door?

I wonder if it's a place to store **small boxes.**

Or does it open to a field of *red flying foxes*?

If I use my imagination it could be anything!

There could be dancing frogs and ducks that sing.

And the **bees would buzz**,
but they wouldn't sting.

Everything in there could be **big and blue...**

like a big blue fish with big blue shoes,

or a big blue moose reading big blue news.

Maybe it's silly
behind the little red door,
with silly vegetable dinosaurs...

like a Tomato-saurus rex
or a Broccoli-raptor,
and I could play songs
that they would clap for.

Or it might be a room that's upside down,

and everything on the ceiling is now on the ground.

Perhaps it's a door to outer space,

with moons
and planets
and stars we
can chase.

Does it smile and have feelings,
just like me?

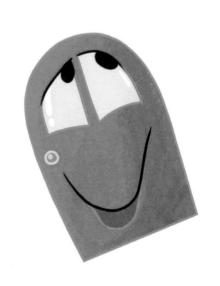  

Like me, does it skip
and climb every tree

and run on the sand and swim in the sea?

I'll say hello, and we can be friends.

And then our adventures
will never end.

Let's count to four and open the door...

What's behind the **little red door**?!

What kind of **world**
do you want to explore?

About the Author   **COY BOWLES**

Coy Bowles writes songs and plays guitar (along with many other instruments) for the Grammy Award-winning Zac Brown Band. Born in Thomaston, Georgia, Coy went on to graduate from the Jazz Studies Program at Georgia State University, then formed his own band, Coy Bowles and the Fellowship. In 2006, he opened for the Zac Brown Band, was asked to join the band full time, and hasn't looked back.

After his success writing lyrics for music, Coy became an accomplished children's book author and has released three middle-grade children's books — *Amy Giggles: Laugh Out Loud, Will Powers: When There's a Will There's a Way*, and *When You're Feeling Sick*, which was published by Penguin Random House. His newest picture book, *Behind the Little Red Door*, was commissioned by the State of Georgia to celebrate the 25th birthday of Georgia's Pre-K Program and will be distributed to 90,000 children. When he's not touring with his books or bands, Coy spends time with his family at home in Georgia. Find his blog and more at coybowles.com and follow him @coybowles.

About the Illustrator   **JOANNA DAVIDOVICH**

Joanna Davidovich was born near Jacksonville, Florida into a family of Ukrainian gymnasts. Skirting the family business, she developed a knack for doodling flamingos wearing sunglasses and somehow made a career out of that. She earned her BFA in Animation from the Savannah College of Art and Design, and graduated in 2005 as salutatorian. She works as an animation artist and illustrator on a great variety of commercials, promos, series, and personal projects. *Behind the Little Red Door* is her first venture into the wonderful world of children's book illustration. She enjoys watching old films and cartoons, singing with her band, Penny Serenade, and just goofing around with her husband and daughter in their Atlanta, Georgia home. Find more of her work at CupOJo.net, and follow her @jothezette.